ALEXANDER AND THE TERRIBLE, HORRIBLE, NO GOOD, VERY BAD DAY

~ A Musical ~

Based on the book by
JUDITH VIORST

Book and Lyrics by
JUDITH VIORST

Music by
SHELLY MARKHAM

Stage directions by
NICK OLCOTT

Based on the original production at the
John F. Kennedy Center for the Performing Arts

Dramatic Publishing
Woodstock, Illinois • England • Australia • New Zealand

*** NOTICE ***

©MCMXCIX
Book and Lyrics by JUDITH VIORST
Music by SHELLY MARKHAM

Based on the book by
JUDITH VIORST

For inquiries concerning all other rights, contact:
Selma Luttinger, Robert A. Freedman Dramatic Agency, Inc.,
1501 Broadway, Suite 2310, New York NY 10036
Phone: (212) 840-5760

ISBN 0-87129-979-8

ALEXANDER AND THE TERRIBLE, HORRIBLE, NO GOOD, VERY BAD DAY was commissioned by the John F. Kennedy Center for the Performing Arts in 1998 and was first produced at the Kennedy Center's Theater Lab on November 27, 1998. The production was directed by Nick Olcott and included the following artists:

CAST

KATE KILEY, RANDY KRAVIS, CARLYNCIA S. PECK,
CLEO REGINALD PIZANA, LYNNE STREETER,
JOSH THELIN, ANDREW ROSS WYNN

PRODUCTION STAFF and CREW

Music Director . . . . GEORGE FULGINITI-SHAKAR
Choreographer. . . . . SANDRA L. HOLLOWAY
Set Designer . . . . JOSEPH B. MUSUMECI JR.
Costume Designer. . . . . ROSEMARY PARDEE
Lighting Designer . . . . LYNN JOSLIN
Casting. . . . . BHK ARTS CONSULTANTS
Assistant Director . . . . BONNIE GERMANN
Properties Artisan . . . . DREAMA J. GREAVES
Orchestrator. . . . . BOB CHRISTIANSON
Production Stage Mgr . JOHN "SCOOTER" KRATTENMAKER

ALEXANDER AND THE TERRIBLE, HORRIBLE, NO GOOD, VERY BAD DAY

A Musical in One Act
For 4 Men and 3 Women playing several roles

CHARACTERS*

ALEXANDER . . . . . . 6 years old (can go up to 7, with his brothers growing younger or older accordingly)

ENSEMBLE #1 . . . . Also plays Nick (Alexander's 9-year-old brother) and Albert Moyo (same age as Alexander)

ENSEMBLE #2 . . . . Also plays Anthony (Alexander's 11-year-old brother) and Becky (same age as Alexander)

ENSEMBLE #3 . . . . Also plays Audrey and Philip Parker (both same age as Alexander)

ENSEMBLE #4 . . . Also plays Paul (same age as Alexander)

MOTHER . . . . Also plays Mrs. Dickens

FATHER . . . . Also plays Dr. Fields and the Shoe Salesman

*All characters can be played by adult actors: the children by actors in their 20s, the adults by actors in their 40s.

SET

The set consists of whatever arrangement allows for a fluid transition in and out of several different locations. Six rolling chairs, one rolling table, and a rolling bed can easily fulfill most of the play's needs. A large rolling copy machine, basically a box big enough to accomodate two actors, is necessary for the office scene. The rest of the physical world is played by the four Ensemble actors.

The play takes place over the course of one day in the life of a middle-class American first- or second-grader with a mother, father, two older brothers, and a finely honed sense of injustice. He NEVER laughs but we hope that everyone else will.

MUSIC AND UNDERSCORING

1A. "Overture"

1B. "PROLOGUE UNDERSCORE"—"If I Were in Charge of the World" snippet

1C. "PROLOGUE UNDERSCORE"—"If I Were" snippet

1D. "PROLOGUE UNDERSCORE"—"If I Were" snippet

1E. "PROLOGUE UNDERSCORE"—"If I Were" snippet

1F. "PROLOGUE UNDERSCORE"—"If I Were" snippet

1G. "PROLOGUE UNDERSCORE"—"If I Were" snippet

1H. "If I Were in Charge of the World" Opener

2A. "Sleepy" Music

2B. "Wake-up" Music–1

2C. "Wake-up" Music–2

2D. "Morning" Music

3. "Lady, Lady" Song

4A. "Baby Sister" Song—False Start–1 (through first line of song)

4B. "Baby Sister" Song—False Start–2 (halfway through second line of song)

4C. "Baby Sister" Song—False Start–3 (through end of second line and bear growl)

4D. "Baby Sister" Song—the whole thing

5. "Lizzie Pitofsky" Song

6A. "Mother Doesn't Want a Dog" Song—False Start (through end of second line)

6B. "Mother Doesn't Want a Dog" Song—the whole thing

7. "Disappointment" Music

8. "Soccer Game" Music

9. "Tag" Music

10A. "Hand-walking" Music—Philip

10B. "Hand-walking" Music—Albert

10C.   "Hand-walking" Music—Paul
11.   "Mother's Dessert" Music
12A.   "Australia" Song
12B.   "Australia" Play-off Music (Dark)
12C.   "Australia" Play-off Music
13A.   "Shoes" Music
13B.   "Shoes"
13C.   "Presentation" Music
13D.   "Shoes" Play-off Music
14.   "Copier" Music
15.   "Bored-dance" Music
16.   "Cell Phone" Music
17.   "Australia"—Final Play-off Music
18.   "Sweetest of Nights and the Finest of Days"
       Intro and Song
19.   "Australia"—Finale Music
20.   "Bows"—"If I Were" Song—last verse only

ALEXANDER AND THE TERRIBLE, HORRIBLE, NO GOOD, VERY BAD DAY

PROLOGUE

House to half. "OVERTURE" (1A)

(One by one, the ENSEMBLE ACTORS run on stage. They are setting a trap for ALEXANDER, who they know will come by this way. When they spot him, they hide. ALEXANDER storms on to center. He is clearly in a vile mood. The four ENSEMBLE ACTORS surround him. The music stops.)

ENSEMBLE #1. Dear Alexander: A dog thought I was a tree. So he went to the bathroom on me. It was a terrible day.

(MUSIC—"IF I WERE IN CHARGE OF THE WORLD" snippet (1B). ALEXANDER tries to escape, but kids head him off at the pass. The music stops.)

ENSEMBLE #2. Dear Alexander: When I went to get my allergy shot I stubbed my toe by accident. On my way back from the allergy doctor two quarters fell out of the hole I have in my jacket. The barber gave me the ugliest haircut you ever saw in your life. This has been a terrible, horrible day.

(MUSIC—"IF I WERE" snippet (1C). Again ALEXANDER tries to escape. Again they surround him. Music stops.)

ENSEMBLE #3. Dear Alexander: I had a hamster named Fluffy. She died last January. I had a hamster named Stinko. He died last May. I got a whole new hamster, but he died this afternoon and I'm having a terrible, horrible, no good day.

(MUSIC—"IF I WERE" snippet (1D). Once again the attempted escape. Once again he is stopped. Music stops.)

ENSEMBLE #4. Dear Alexander: I had fifty-two chances to get the ball in the basket. My basketball missed the basket fifty-two times. They said I could have some more chances but I don't want any more chances. It's been a terrible, horrible, no good, very bad day.

(MUSIC—"IF I WERE" snippet (1E). Another attempt. Another defeat. Music stops.)

ENSEMBLE #1. Dear Alexander: They said if I didn't finish my oatmeal this morning I wasn't getting any dessert tonight. I didn't think they'd remember. They did. I didn't think I'd care THAT MUCH. I did. So everybody else had strawberry shortcake, and I had a terrible, I had a horrible, I had a no good, I had a very bad day.

(MUSIC—"IF I WERE" snippet (1F). Same business. Music stops.)

ENSEMBLE #4. Dear Alexander: Somebody called me fatso and when anyone calls me fatso it's a terrible, horrible, no good, very bad day.

(MUSIC—"IF I WERE" snippet (1G). This time ALEXANDER attempts to escape into the audience, but realizes for the first time that they are there. He pulls back from them and is now well and truly surrounded by the ENSEMBLE ACTORS. Music stops.)

ENSEMBLE #3. Dear Alexander: My little sister isn't allowed to go in my bedroom. Ever! She went anyway. My sister also isn't allowed to open my gerbil cage. Ever! She opened it anyway. And here's what I wish: I wish I could lose my sister and find my gerbil. And here's what I am having: I'm having a terrible, horrible, no good, very bad day.

(MUSIC—"IF I WERE" Opener—Intro and Song (1H). The intro starts under "I'M HAVING," plays under the next speech, and leads into ALEXANDER's beginning of the song "IF I WERE IN CHARGE OF THE WORLD.")

ENSEMBLE #1. Dear Alexander: If I were in charge of the world, I would fix it so people would never have a terrible...

ADD ENSEMBLE #2. ...horrible...
ADD ENSEMBLE #3. ...no good...

ADD ENSEMBLE #4. ... very bad day!

(ALEXANDER now turns to the audience and begins song "IF I WERE IN CHARGE OF THE WORLD." Choreographed movement should accompany this number.)

ALEXANDER *(sings)*.
If I were in charge of the world
I'd cancel oatmeal ...

ENSEMBLE #3 *(sings)*.
Monday mornings ...

ENSEMBLE #2 *(sings)*.
Allergy shots ...

ENSEMBLE #4 *(sings)*.
And also Sara Steinberg.

ENSEMBLE #1 *(sings)*.
If I were in charge of the world ...

ENSEMBLE #2 *(sings)*.
There'd be brighter night-lights ...

ENSEMBLE #3 *(sings)*.
Healthier hamsters ...

ENSEMBLE #4 *(sings)*.
And basketball baskets forty-eight inches lower.

ALEXANDER *(sings)*.
    If I were in charge of the world...

ENSEMBLE #1 *(sings)*.
    You wouldn't have lonely.

ALEXANDER *(sings)*.
    You wouldn't have bedtimes.

ENSEMBLE #2 *(sings)*.
    Or "Don't punch your sister."

ENSEMBLE #3 *(sings)*.
    You wouldn't even have sisters.

ALEXANDER *(sings)*.
    If I were in charge of the world
    A chocolate sundae with whipped cream and nuts
        would be a vegetable.
    And every kind of movie would be G.
    And a person who sometimes forgot to brush,
    And sometimes forgot to flush,
    Would still be allowed to be
    In charge of the world.

ENSEMBLE #3 *(sings)*.
    If I were in charge of the world
    I'd put in more rainbows and leave out all the
        thorns and snakes.

ENSEMBLE #1 *(sings)*.
    I'd put in mermaids and unicorns...

ALEXANDER *(sings).*
>   And leave out splinters, cavities, and stomach
>   aches.

ENSEMBLE #2 *(sings).*
>   I'd put in magic carpets.
>   And I'd put in wishing wells.

ADD ENSEMBLE #1 *(sings).*
>   And I'd put in genies.

ALEXANDER *(sings).*
>   And I'd leave out wars and tornadoes.
>   And leave out dress-up clothes.

ENSEMBLE #4 *(sings).*
>   And good guys getting picked on by the meanies.

ALL TOGETHER *(sings).*
>   If I were in charge of the world...

ALEXANDER *(sings).*
>   There'd be no more raining on soccer games.
>   Or *(yecch)* liver for dinner.

ENSEMBLE #3 *(sings).*
>   And no more playing board games
>   Where you always get to lose

ENSEMBLE #2 *(sings).*
>   And your brother always gets to be the winner.

ALL TOGETHER *(sing).*
> If I were in charge of the world...

ALEXANDER *(sings).*
> There'd be no more staying home at night
> With some bossy old sitter.

ENSEMBLE #4 *(sings).*
> And no more being scolded
> when your cousin...

ENSEMBLE #1. the big pest...

ENSEMBLE #4 *(sings).*
> ...was being so REALLY pesty that you bit her.

ALL TOGETHER *(sing).*
> If I were in charge of the world
> A chocolate sundae with whipped cream and nuts
>   would be a vegetable.
> And every kind of movie would be G.
> And a person who sometimes forgot to brush,
> And sometimes forgot to flush,
> Would still be allowed to be
> Would still be allowed to be
> Would still be allowed to be
> In charge of the world.

(End of number. After the applause:)

ALL FOUR ENSEMBLE ACTORS PLUS ALEXANDER (*singing-speaking in unison*). If we were in charge of the world we'd fix it so people would never have a terrible, horrible, no good, very bad day.

(*MOTHER and FATHER enter and look at the KIDS. FATHER points at his watch or a clock. Suddenly, the KIDS make the sound of alarm clocks of all types going off all over the place. They exit, making the clock sounds. Maybe one of them is the voice of a radio announcer saying something like: "This is radio WTHNGVB (or KTHNGVB) saying, It's time for school, kids. Wakey, wakey, up and at 'em." MOTHER calls upstairs to the boys as the ENSEMBLE exits.*)

MOTHER. Up time. Come on, everybody, out of bed. Anthony, Nick, ALEXANDER!!

(*Silence. She turns to FATHER, who also calls up the stairs.*)

FATHER. Hey, guys. I want to hear some action up there.

(*A couple of beats and then a burst of noise as NICK and ANTHONY enter, yawning and scratching.*)

MOTHER. Good morning, Nick. (*She gives him a kiss.*) Good morning, Anthony. (*She tries to kiss him too*). So, where's Alexander?
NICK. We traded him for two pairs of roller blades.
ANTHONY. Wrong, Nick. They said that he was only worth ONE pair of roller blades.

NICK. Actually, he moved to the zoo with all the other animals.

ANTHONY. No, he went downtown to a store to buy a new face.

FATHER. Hey, you comedians, can we please get a straight answer? Is your brother awake?

NICK. Well, I'll tell you—Peter Pan flew in his window, and took him to Never Never Land last night. And now *(he pretends to sob)* we're never never gonna see him again.

ANTHONY *(also pretending to sob loudly)*. Never never.

NICK *(sobbing even louder)*. Never never nev—

MOTHER. Okay, enough. I better go wake him up.

(MOTHER exits as ANTHONY and NICK break up at their joke. FATHER herds them off in the opposite direction and exits. "SLEEPY" MUSIC (2A) begins as EN-SEMBLE ACTORS roll on ALEXANDER's bed and scatter his toys on the floor: a train, a drum, and a skateboard. ALEXANDER is in the bed, blankets pulled over his head, only a tuft of unruly hair showing. MOTHER enters as the ENSEMBLE ACTORS exit. "SLEEPY" music fades when bed is in place and before MOTHER delivers line.)

MOTHER *(sweetly)*. Alexander, time to get up.

(No sound or movement from ALEXANDER.)

MOTHER *(firmly)*. Wake up, Alexander.

(No sound or movement. MOTHER starts shaking him. ALEXANDER moans but doesn't budge.)

MOTHER *(yanking off the blankets).* Alexander, you have exactly— *(She looks at her watch.)* —four minutes to get washed, tooth-brushed, dressed, and down in the kitchen. *(She shakes him again.)* Speak, so I know you heard me.

ALEXANDER *(groaningly).* I heard you.

(He pulls the covers back over himself. MOTHER pulls the covers back off and gives him a gentle-but-firm whack on the bottom. She exits. "WAKE-UP" MUSIC–1 (2B) begins on MOTHER's exit. ALEXANDER sits up in bed, rubs his eyes, stretches, pauses for a moment as an idea strikes him, then starts poking inside his mouth looking for something. "WAKE-UP" MUSIC–1 fades before he delivers next line.)

ALEXANDER. My gum! I had all this gum! Where's my gum?

(He searches through the bedclothes, searches some more, shrugs, gives up the search. He scratches his head with both hands and suddenly feels the gum in his hair. He slowly pulls his fingers away from his hair and we see him staring at large gobs of gum now stuck to his fingers. The ACTOR should pantomime the gum.)

ALEXANDER. Oh, yuck!

(*He first tries to get the gum off one hand with the other hand. It sags between the two. He succeeds in getting it all on one hand, but then tries to get it off. It sticks both his hands together. Finally he wipes his gummy hands on his pajamas. He gets out of bed. He stumbles over his toy train. He picks it up, glares at it accusingly, and tosses it onto the bed. He starts away from his bed and steps on his skateboard, which flies up to his chest. He catches it and falls to the floor. He rises slowly from the floor, glares at the skateboard, and marches toward the bed. On the way he steps into his drum, putting his foot through the drum head. He turns to the audience and speaks to them with heart-felt emotion.*)

ALEXANDER. I hate mornings.

(*"WAKE-UP" MUSIC—2 (2C) plays to cover this next transition. The ENSEMBLE ACTORS enter with his clothes. ALEXANDER starts to unbutton his pajamas, then—taking note of the audience—modestly moves to behind the bed quilt, which two of the ENSEMBLE ACTORS hold up for him. As he dresses, another ENSEMBLE ACTOR becomes a bathroom sink. Wearing a faucet mounted on a baseball cap, he demonstrates the cold tap by pantomiming turning it on and off and testing it with his hand. It's fine. Then he demonstrates the hot tap, but the hot water burns his hand and he blows on his fingers. He then clasps his arms in front of him in a circular shape to form the sink and kneels as ALEXANDER, now dressed, emerges from behind the quilt. One ENSEMBLE ACTOR hands ALEXANDER a sweater, which he carries toward the bathroom. Another ENSEM-*

*BLE ACTOR becomes the door to the bathroom. ALEX-
ANDER opens the door and enters the bathroom. The
door slams on ALEXANDER's back and chortles to itself. ALEXANDER glares at it, then drapes his sweater
over the head of the actor playing the sink and turns on
the faucet. The actor playing the sink reacts with dis-
pleasure to the sweater, then makes the sound of running
water. "WAKE-UP" music fades as ALEXANDER starts
to sing-chant.)*

ALEXANDER *(sings or chants as he pantomimes the
washcloth and soap).*
> It just takes a second to wash my face, wash my face,
> wash my face.
> It just takes a second to wash my face,
> Early in the morning.

*(He dries his hands on his shirt, then pantomimes pick-
ing up a toothbrush and putting toothpaste on it. He
sings or chants as he pantomimes brushing his teeth.)*

> It just takes a second to brush my teeth, brush my
> teeth, brush my teeth.
> It just takes a second to brush my teeth,
> Early in the morning.

*(He pantomimes spitting toothpaste into the "sink." The
actor playing the sink reacts with distaste and decides to
get even. ALEXANDER wipes his mouth on his shirt
sleeve and dries his hands on his shirt as he sings or
chants the following, then reaches for the sweater.)*

It just takes a second to put on my sweater,
   put on my sweater, put on ...

(At that moment the actor playing the sink dumps the sweater from his head into what would be the running water. ALEXANDER screams with anguish as the ENSEMBLE ACTORS make the sound of a splash and the SINK chuckles to itself.)

ALEXANDER. No! No! No!

(ALEXANDER grabs the sweater and turns off the sink with anger. The actor playing the sink makes choking noises, then settles into a vindictive drip. ALEXANDER tries to open the bathroom door. It resists his efforts twice but the third time flies open and ALEXANDER comes pitching out into his bedroom, clutching the soaked sweater in one hand. The ENSEMBLE ACTORS exit, with the sink giving the door a "high five." ALEXANDER glares at them as they retreat, then moves downstage to speak directly to the audience. Behind him ENSEMBLE ACTORS remove the bed.)

ALEXANDER. I went to sleep with gum in my mouth and now there's gum in my hair and when I got out of bed this morning I tripped on the skateboard and by mistake I dropped my sweater in the sink while the water was running and I could tell it was going to be a terrible, horrible, no good, very bad day.

(If the audience begins speaking the terrible, horrible, etc., along with ALEXANDER, he can react with sur-

*prise and delight. So there are people out there who un-
derstand his plight, even if no one in his world does.*

*ALEXANDER exits and "MORNING" MUSIC (2D) cov-
ers transition to breakfast as NICK and ANTHONY roll
on the table and three chairs. There are three big boxes
of cereal, three bowls, and three spoons on the table.
NICK and ANTHONY take their places as ALEXANDER
enters. "MORNING" music fades before NICK speaks.)*

NICK *(to ANTHONY)*. They don't even want him in Never
Never Land.

ANTHONY *(shaking his head)*. Never, never. *(Puts his
hand in his cereal box and pulls out a car kit.)* Whoa,
look at the prize in my cereal box. A Corvette Sting Ray
car kit. This is goooood.

NICK *(rummaging through his cereal box)*. Wait! I bet I
got something good too. *(Keeps rummaging.)* I'm feeling
it, I'm feeling it, it's here, it's right here, it's... *(Pulls
out a ring.)* Cool! A Junior Undercover Agent code ring.

ALEXANDER. Mine's gonna be the best. You'll see. *(He
digs his hand into the box as far as it will go. He shakes
it. Peers into it. Then he lifts the box up over his face
and tears open the bottom, whereupon all the cereal
spills out on him and the table. He hunts frantically and
fruitlessly for his prize.)*

NICK *(tauntingly)*. So what did you get, Alexander?

ALEXANDER. I'm looking.

ANTHONY. Yeah, Alexander, what prize did you get?

ALEXANDER. I'm still looking.

(MOTHER and FATHER enter as ALEXANDER continues his search.)

MOTHER. Alexander, you're making a major mess here. Did you find what you wanted?

(ALEXANDER looks up with his hands filled with cereal. He speaks to the audience.)

ALEXANDER. All I found in my breakfast cereal box was—breakfast cereal.

(The FAMILY looks at ALEXANDER and freezes.)

ALEXANDER. I think I'll move to Australia.

(The FAMILY looks at each other, then back to ALEXANDER, then exits with table and two of the chairs as the OTHER ENSEMBLE ACTORS enter making the sounds of car horns and traffic. ALEXANDER walks to the center. ONE ACTOR takes ALEXANDER's chair and runs it all over the stage, playing as if it were a car. The ACTOR then runs the chair into the back of ALEXANDER's knees, bumping him into a sitting position on the chair. The ACTOR honks at him and runs off. ALEXANDER is center stage on a chair. He is in the middle of the back seat in the car-pool car. He pantomimes putting on his seat belt.)

ALEXANDER *(speaking to audience).* In the car pool, Mrs. Gibson let Becky have a seat by the window. *(Leaning forward and addressing an imaginary BECKY in the front seat.)* Not fair! *(Speaking again to audience.)* Audrey and Elliott got seats by the window too. *(He sequentially turns to the left and the right and addresses an imaginary AUDREY and ELLIOTT.)* Not fair! Not fair! *(Speaking to audience.)* I said I was being scrunched. *(ALEXANDER crosses his arms and presses his elbows and grunts and groans, and gives a good imitation of being scrunched.)* I said I was being smushed. *(ALEXANDER clutches his head and presses his knees together and grunts and groans some more, giving a good imitation of being smushed.)* I said, if I don't get a seat by the window I am going to be *(he leans forward and gives a good imitation of throwing up on BECKY's head in the front seat)* carsick. *(Beat. He looks around.)* No one even answered. *(He pantomimes undoing his seat belt.)* I could tell it was going to be a terrible, horrible, no good, very bad day.

(Again, if the audience speaks the terrible, horribles with him, he should acknowledge their support. Suddenly, the ENSEMBLE ACTORS rush on with chairs, each making a different school bell sound. They form the classroom, and ALEXANDER pushes his chair to join them. The ENSEMBLE ACTORS are now in the costumes to be ALEXANDER's classmates ALBERT, BECKY, AUDREY, and PAUL. MRS. DICKENS enters.)

MRS. DICKENS. So, class, what has everyone drawn today?

(All the CHILDREN put up their hands to be called upon. Each pantomimes holding a picture. MRS. DICKENS calls on her pet.)

MRS. DICKENS. Audrey?

(AUDREY walks forward and pantomimes handing MRS. DICKENS her drawing. MRS. DICKENS pantomimes taking it from her and looking at it.)

MRS. DICKENS. Thank you, Audrey. *(Scrutinizes the drawing.)* I see a red house, and some dark storm clouds, and—hmmm, what are these?

AUDREY. Polka dot raindrops.

(The other KIDS snigger until MRS. DICKENS approves.)

MRS. DICKENS. Oh, yes. I see what you mean. Polka dot raindrops. Good imagination.

(She hands the drawing back to AUDREY, who proudly prances to her seat as the others beg to be called on.)

MRS. DICKENS. All right. Albert.

(ALBERT comes forward and pantomimes handing her his picture. MRS. DICKENS studies it.)

MRS. DICKENS. Well, this looks a lot like, a lot like— five heads on one body.

(The kids snigger.)

ALBERT. It's a picture of my family.

(The kids guffaw until MRS. DICKENS speaks.)

MRS. DICKENS. Uh, huh. Your … family. Very good imagination.

(ALBERT pantomimes taking his drawing back, showing it to the class, and returns to his seat.)

MRS. DICKENS. Alexander?

(She reaches out her hand to take ALEXANDER's drawing. He stands and starts to give it to her, then puts it behind his back. She beckons impatiently and he reluctantly hands it over. MRS. DICKENS studies it, turns it over on the other side, ALEXANDER pantomimes turning it back to the first side.)

MRS. DICKENS. I may be missing something here, but I don't see any picture. *(Holding it up to the class.)* Class, do you see any picture?
ALL KIDS EXCEPT ALEXANDER. No.
MRS. DICKENS. Didn't you do a drawing today, Alexander?

(ALEXANDER nods his head vigorously.)

MRS. DICKENS. Where is it?

(ALEXANDER whispers something inaudible in her ear.)

MRS. DICKENS. It's right HERE? *(She studies the drawing again.)* WHAT'S right here?

(ALEXANDER again whispers in her ear.)

MRS. DICKENS. An invisible castle. You drew an INVISIBLE castle?

(ALEXANDER nods his head vigorously.)

MRS. DICKENS. Well, that's TOO much imagination, Alexander. Much too much imagination.

(MRS. DICKENS pantomimes handing the drawing back to ALEXANDER. The CLASS stifles its giggles, as ALEXANDER skulks back to his seat. PAUL dashes forward without being called on.)

MRS. DICKENS *(pantomiming taking PAUL's proffered drawing and examining it)*. Now, Paul, this is a WONDERFUL...

(MRS. DICKENS exits, taking the picture with her. PAUL does a little celebration dance, and the children exit, making the sounds of school bells as they go. ALEXANDER moves downstage and speaks to the audience.)

ALEXANDER. At school Mrs. Dickens liked Paul's picture of the sailboat better than my picture of the invisible castle. At counting time she said I left out sixteen. Who needs sixteen? I could tell it was going to be a terrible, horrible, no good, very bad day.

(Again he acknowledges any support he receives from the audience. The ENSEMBLE enter again, making the sound of school bells as they take their places in the classroom. MRS. DICKENS enters.)

MRS. DICKENS. All right, class. Let's hear the songs you picked to sing at the school concert. Audrey, why don't you start.

"LADY, LADY" SONG (3)

AUDREY *(coming to the front of the class and singing sweetly).*
 Lady, lady, in the valley.
 Lady, lady, on the hill.
 Come and tell me all your stories.
 Lady, lady, say you will.

 Tell them in the summer, lady.
 Tell them when the snow is deep.
 Tell them in the morning, lady.
 Tell them when I go to sleep.

 Tell them serious and silly.
 Tell them, lady, small and grand.
 You can even tell them scary
 If you'll sit and hold my hand.

Tell of things around the corner.
Tell of things across the sea.
Tell of dwarfs and dragons, lady.
Tell of boys and girls like me.

Tell of pigs and princes, lady.
Tell of buses, blimps, and birds.
Make me cry and make me giggle.
Fill my head and heart with words.

Someday I will be a grown-up.
Someday I'll make stories too.
If you'll just be patient, lady,
Someday I'll tell mine to you.

(*During the song, ALL CHILDREN, including ALEXAN-
DER, get caught up in the song's fairy-tale fantasy, and
act it out. This could be lightly choreographed. The only
difference is that the other kids seem to know what to do
immediately. ALEXANDER is always behind the rest.
They all applaud AUDREY as the song ends. Wait for
audience to applaud too.*)

MRS. DICKENS. Beautifully sung, Audrey. Now, Becky
and Alexander, you were going to sing something together?

(*PAUL, AUDREY, and ALBERT pull to a corner of the
classroom while BECKY tries to negotiate with MRS.
DICKENS in another corner. We don't hear BECKY
speak, but she clearly is objecting to this duet with*

ALEXANDER. Meanwhile ALEXANDER, standing center, is practicing the song to himself.)

PAUL *(whispering to ALBERT)*. Becky is singing with Alexander?

ALBERT *(whispering to PAUL)*. Looks like it. Poor her.

AUDREY *(whispering to ALBERT)*. You're not kidding, poor her. How come she's doing this?

ALBERT *(whispering to AUDREY)*. Mrs. Dickens asked her to. She said our school concert should have a duet.

PAUL *(whispering to ALBERT)*. A DUET?

AUDREY *(whispering to PAUL)*. That's two singers singing the same song.

PAUL *(forgetting to whisper)*. I know what a duet is. But Becky and Alexander aren't two singers. They're one singer and one...

MRS. DICKENS. Hush, everybody. Becky and Alexander, you may begin.

(BECKY gives MRS. DICKENS one more pleading look, but the teacher gestures for her to begin. BECKY does so—against her will. "BABY SISTER" SONG—FALSE START-1 (4A).)

BECKY & ALEXANDER *(singing together, with ALEXANDER loud and off key)*.
   I love love love my brand-new baby sister...

(Music stops as MRS. DICKENS delivers line.)

MRS. DICKENS *(interrupting)*. No, no. Try to find the tune, Alexander.

"BABY SISTER" SONG—FALSE START-2 (4B)

BECKY & ALEXANDER *(starting again, ALEXANDER trying hard but still loud and off key).*
> I love love love my brand-new baby sister.
> I'd never feed her to a—

(Music stops as MRS. DICKENS delivers line.)

MRS. DICKENS *(interrupting).* If you can't find the tune, Alexander, please sing softer.

"BABY SISTER" SONG—FALSE START-3 (4C)

BECKY & ALEXANDER *(starting again, ALEXANDER singing softer but still off key).*
> I love love love my brand-new baby sister.
> I'd never feed her to a hungry bear.

(ALEXANDER gets carried away and makes a huge bear growl and dramatic bear-claw gesture. Music stops as MRS. DICKENS delivers line.)

MRS. DICKENS *(interrupting again).* Stop. Let's let Becky do this one alone, Alexander, while you think of another song to sing.

"BABY SISTER" SONG (4D)

BECKY.
> I love love love my brand-new baby sister.

I'd never feed her to a hungry bear.
I'd never (no! no! no!)
Put her outside in the snow
And by mistake forget I put her there.

I'd never want to flush her down the toilet.
I'd never want to drop her on her head.
I'm only asking if
She by mistake fell off a cliff
The next time we could get a dog instead?

(The CHILDREN clap enthusiastically. Give audience a chance to clap. Throughout the clapping, ALEXANDER pouts.)

MRS. DICKENS. Well now. That was very ... tuneful.

(PAUL charges to the front without waiting to be called on.)

MRS. DICKENS. So, okay, Paul, what are you going to sing?

PAUL. It's a song about a girl named Lizzie Pitofsky.

ALEXANDER. A GIRL. You're going to sing a song about a GIRL?

PAUL. Quiet, Alexander.

ALEXANDER *(appealing to ALBERT for support)*. But he's going to sing a song about a GIRL!

AUDREY. Quiet, Alexander

ALEXANDER. But ...

MRS. DICKENS. Alexander, let's just listen to the song.

*("LIZZIE PITOFSKY" SONG (5). Some choreographed
gestures and movements, exaggeratedly heartfelt, work
well here.)*

PAUL *(stands before the class and sings).*
> I can't get enoughsky
> Of Lizzie Pitofsky.
> I love her so much that it hurts.
> I want her so terrible
> I'd give her my gerbil
> Plus twenty-two weeks of desserts.
>
> I know that it's lovesky
> 'Cause Lizzie Pitofsky
> Is turning me into a saint.
> I smell like a rose,
> I've stopped picking my nose,
> And I practically never say ain't.
>
> I don't push and shovesky
> 'Cause Lizzie Pitofsky
> Likes boys who are gentle and kind.
> I'm not throwing rocks
> And I'm changing my socks
> (And to tell you the truth I don't mind.)
>
> So put tacks in my shoes,
> Feed me vinegar juice,
> And do other mean bad awful stuffsky.
> But promise me this:
> I won't die without kiss-
> Ing my glorious Lizzie Pitofsky.

(EVERYONE except ALEXANDER applauds enthusiastically. The audience applauds. Then the ACTORS freeze as ALEXANDER comes to center and addresses the audience.)

ALEXANDER. Kissing! Yuck!

(They unfreeze as he returns to his seat.)

MRS. DICKENS. Nicely done, Paul.

(PAUL bows and takes his seat.)

MRS. DICKENS. Now I believe it's Albert's turn. Are you ready?

ALBERT. I'm ready.

("MOTHER DOESN'T WANT A DOG" SONG (6A)— FALSE START)

ALBERT *(comes to front of class and sings).*
    Mother doesn't want a dog.
    Mother says they smell.

(ALBERT holds his nose to indicate smelly. ALEXANDER raises and frantically waves his hand, making so much fuss that ALBERT stops singing. Music stops as ALEXANDER delivers line.)

ALEXANDER. That's the "another" song you told me to think of. I could sing that song.

(ALBERT, his fingers still holding his nose, turns toward MRS. DICKENS.)

MRS. DICKENS. I'm sorry, Albert. *(Removing ALBERT's fingers from his nose and sighing.)* Look, would it be all right if Alexander sang with you?

ALBERT. Does he have to?

MRS. DICKENS. It would be really nice if you let him. Okay?

ALBERT. I guess.

"MOTHER DOESN'T WANT A DOG" SONG (6B)

ALBERT & ALEXANDER *(sing, with ALEXANDER singing enthusiastically, but loudly and off key).*
> Mother doesn't want a dog.
> Mother says they smell,

MRS. DICKENS *(speaking over their singing).* Softer, Alexander.

ALBERT & ALEXANDER *(sing; ALEXANDER still enthusiastic, still off key, singing softer).*
> And never sit when you say sit,
> Or even when you yell.

(ALEXANDER gets carried away and yells the last phrase.)

MRS. DICKENS *(speaking over the song).* Still softer, Alexander.

ALBERT & ALEXANDER *(sing; ALEXANDER singing even softer, still off key).*
>   And when you come home late at night
>   And there is ice and snow
>   You have to go back out because
>   The dumb dog has to go.

(ALEXANDER again gets loud as he tries to impress this clever line on the class.)

MRS. DICKENS. Alexander, shhhh. I mean, really shhh.

ALBERT & ALEXANDER *(only ALBERT sings; ALEXANDER silently mouths the words).*
>   Mother doesn't want a dog.
>   Mother says they shed,
>   And always let the strangers in
>   And bark at friends instead,
>   And do disgraceful things on rugs,
>   And track mud on the floor,
>   And flop upon your bed at night
>   And snore their doggy snore.

(Again ALEXANDER gets carried away and makes a big snoring sound.)

MRS. DICKENS *(over them).* Shhhhhhhhh!!!!!

(During this next part of the number and through to the end, ALBERT and ALEXANDER could do a few simple dance steps, with ALBERT the more competent, of course.)

ALBERT & ALEXANDER (*sing, but ALBERT is doing the actual singing while ALEXANDER is only mouthing the words*).

> **Mother doesn't want a dog.**
> **She's making a mistake.**
> **Because, more than a dog, I think**
> **She will not want this snake.**

(*ALBERT pulls out a fake snake and shakes it at everyone. AUDREY screams, BECKY acts disgusted, PAUL breaks up. ALEXANDER grabs the snake from ALBERT and tries to get an even bigger reaction from the class.*)

ALEXANDER (*without music, sings very loudly and off key*).

> **She will not want,**
> **She will not want,**
> **She will not want**
> **This snake.**

(*The others look at ALEXANDER with disgust and disbelief. He stops as they all leave the classroom, shaking their heads. ALBERT is the last, grabbing the snake back from ALEXANDER. MRS. DICKENS comes to ALEXANDER.*)

MRS. DICKENS. Too loud, Alexander. Way, way, way too loud. (*She exits.*)

(*"DISAPPOINTMENT" MUSIC (7) covers transition to soccer game and fades when bells sound. The ENSEMBLE make the sounds of school bells and move whatever set pieces it takes to take us outside onto the playground. ALBERT and PAUL enter and begin pantomiming kicking a soccer ball around.)*

PAUL. Over here, Albert.

(ALBERT pantomimes kicking a soccer ball high in the air to PAUL, who bounces it off his knees, his head, the backs of his heels. These very showy soccer moves are much more easily accomplished with an imaginary ball. PHILIP arrives at the playground as this is happening.)

PHILIP. Good one, Paul.

Center stage

(PAUL pantomimes kicking the ball to PHILIP. "SOCCER GAME" MUSIC (8) begins.)

ALEXANDER. Hey, Philip, kick one to me.

(PHILIP kicks it instead to ALBERT, who kicks it to PAUL, as ALEXANDER tries to get in on the game.)

ALEXANDER. Come on, guys, kick it to me.

(PAUL kicks it to PHILIP, who drives it across the field. ALEXANDER tries to block the drive. PHILIP kicks it to ALBERT, and it goes right through ALEXANDER's legs.)

PAUL, PHILIP, & ALBERT. Through your legs! Through your legs!

(ALBERT kicks it across to PHILIP, and ALEXANDER tries to intercept the kick, but he misses the ball completely and falls on his back.)

PAUL & ALBERT *(as they help ALEXANDER up)*. Alexander!!!

ALEXANDER. I'm okay, I'm okay. *(To PHILIP, who now has the ball.)* Come ON. I said kick one to me.

("SOCCER GAME" music fades when PHILIP kicks the ball.

At a sign from PAUL, PHILIP kicks the ball far and high, way over ALEXANDER's head. They laugh while he runs offstage to get it, then PAUL huddles with ALBERT and PHILIP.)

PAUL. Game change. Game change. *(Swatting PHILIP on his shoulder.)* Okay, Philip, we're playing tag and you just got to be "it."

("TAG" MUSIC (9) begins when PAUL tags PHILIP.

ALBERT and PAUL scatter as PHILIP tries to decide who to go after, first one, then the other, finally tagging ALBERT. ALBERT is chasing them when ALEXANDER re-enters and sees what is happening. ALBERT finally tags PAUL, and ALEXANDER pantomimes putting down the ball to join in the game. He runs over and thrusts himself in PAUL's face.)

ALEXANDER Tag ME! Tag ME!

PAUL. No! I'm after Philip! Hey, Philip! You can't get away.

(*PAUL continues chasing PHILIP, who keeps hiding behind ALBERT, who in turn keeps hiding behind PHILIP, such that PAUL can never get his intended target. ALEXANDER, meanwhile, keeps trying to get tagged by PAUL, who studiously avoids him. Finally, determined to get in the game, ALEXANDER deliberately bumps into PAUL.*)

ALEXANDER. Okay, you tagged me, Paul. Now I'M "it."

(*ALBERT and PHILIP start to run away from him, but stop as soon as PAUL speaks. "TAG" music fades out as PAUL speaks.*)

PAUL. I'm tired of tag.
ALBERT. Me too.
PHILIP. Me too. ~sit down~
ALEXANDER. Me too. Me too. What'll we play now?
PHILIP (*talking to PAUL and ALBERT*). Hey, you guys, hold up my legs and I'll show you how I can walk on my hands.

(*PAUL and ALBERT each hold up one of PHILIP's legs.*)

PHILIP. Ready.   ~cross stage~

(*"HAND-WALKING" MUSIC (10A) begins. PHILIP does some fancy hand-walking.*)

PHILIP *(waving one hand).* Hi. *(Waving other hand.)* Hi.

(ALL KIDS, including ALEXANDER, cheer him on. Music ends when PHILIP is done with hand-walking.)

ALBERT. My turn now.

(ALEXANDER tries to hold one of ALBERT's legs, but PAUL pushes him out of the way. PHILIP and PAUL hold up ALBERT's legs.)

ALBERT. Ready.

("HAND-WALKING" MUSIC (10B) begins. ALBERT does some fancy hand-walking.)

ALBERT *(waving one hand).* Hello. *(Waving other hand.)* Hello.

(The KIDS cheer him on. Music ends when ALBERT is done with hand-walking.)

PAUL. Okay, now me. Wait'll you see what I can do.

(ALEXANDER tries to hold one of PAUL's legs, but PAUL pushes him away. PAUL tries to get up on his own but can't.)

PAUL. Hey, guys!

(PHILIP and ALBERT rush to help PAUL up, pushing ALEXANDER out of the way. They hold PAUL's legs.

"HAND-WALKING" MUSIC (10C) begins. PAUL does whatever hand-walking he can do. It doesn't have to be good. The others cheer him on like a champ, and applaud loudly when he's done. Music ends when PAUL is done hand-walking.)

ALEXANDER. Now ME. Now it's MY turn.

(He starts to go onto his hands, but PAUL stops him.)

PAUL. You don't have a turn. We just need one walker and two holders so we don't need you.

(ALEXANDER stands there glaring at PAUL, outrage warring with hurt and outrage winning.)

ALEXANDER. How come you're being so mean to me? I'm your best friend.

PAUL. You USED to be my best friend. Now Philip is my best friend. And Albert is my next best friend. And you —well, you're only my THIRD best friend.

(PAUL, PHILIP, and ALBERT exchange a special friendship handshake.)

ALEXANDER *(taking a deep breath before letting PAUL have it)*. I hope you sit on a tack. I hope the next time you get a double decker strawberry ice-cream cone the ice cream part falls off the cone part and lands in Australia.

(PAUL steps forward, as if he might punch ALEXAN-DER. He thinks better of it, signals to PHILIP, and leaves. PHILIP signals to ALBERT and leaves. ALBERT has no one to signal to, shakes a finger at ALEXANDER, and leaves. ALEXANDER steps downstage and addresses the audience.)

ALEXANDER. There were two cupcakes in Philip Parker's lunch bag.

PHILIP *(crossing stage holding the cupcakes)*. I love these cupcakes.

ALEXANDER. And Albert got a Hershey bar with almonds.

ALBERT *(crossing stage holding his chocolate bar)*. I love Hershey bars with almonds.

ALEXANDER. And Paul's mother gave him a piece of jelly roll that had little coconut sprinkles on the top.

PAUL *(crossing stage holding the jelly roll)*. I love those little coconut sprinkles.

ALEXANDER. Guess whose mother forgot to put in dessert.

("MOTHER'S DESSERT" MUSIC (11) plays throughout MOTHER's travels across the stage.

MOTHER travels across stage sitting on the rolling table, propelled by ANTHONY and FATHER. She is holding a beautiful dessert, which she reaches out toward ALEXANDER. Just as he tries to take it, she—beginning to eat the dessert herself—is pushed offstage. Music ends. ALEXANDER turns to the audience and enlists their help.)

ALEXANDER. It was a terrible... Come on, you guys, say it with me. It was a terrible... yeah, that's right... horrible... no good... very bad day.

(ALEXANDER jumps up and punches his fist in the air. Just as he does so, the ENSEMBLE make the sound of school bells, and PHILIP and PAUL come running out onto the playground.)

PAUL *(to ALEXANDER)*. Even though you're only my third best friend, you still could come to my house after school if you want.

ALEXANDER. I can't. My mom's taking us all to the dentist—Anthony, Nick, and me. I hate the dentist.

PAUL. You DO? Why? Just because when you go to see him he sticks in that Novocain needle—ooh, owww—

PHILIP. —and then he gets out that drill and it goes bzzzz, bzzzz, bzzzz, and you can feel that bzzzz all the way down to your toes—

PAUL. —and then afterwards your face is all swollen up like a big fat Halloween jack-o'lantern—and everyone else is eating corn on the cob but you can't eat it because it hurts to chew—

PHILIP. —ooooo, it hurts so much—

PAUL. The pain! The pain!

PHILIP. I can't stand it! I can't stand it!

(ALEXANDER looks increasingly terror-stricken, and PAUL and PHILIP exit snickering at ALEXANDER's fear.)

ALEXANDER (*speaking to audience*). I think I'll move to
Australia.

"AUSTRALIA" SONG (12A)

ALEXANDER (*sings*).
My day's been really yuck.
My luck's been all bad luck.
I'm packing up and moving to Australia.
I've just flunked every test.
I'm not my best friend's best.
I think I'm gonna move to Au Au Australia.

Down Under. Down Under.
They call Australia Down Under
Because it's upside down.
When here there's darkest night
It's super-sunshine-bright
In every right-side-up Australia town.

Down Under. Down Under.
They call Australia Down Under
Because it's way down there. *hit a stick*
When here it's sweat sweat sweat
Australia's where folks get
Cool breezes blowing through their underwear.

(*During the number, MOTHER and FATHER, wearing
sunglasses and fanning themselves with palm fans, enter,
and are later joined by the ENSEMBLE, including two
who enter hip-hopping and dressed as a kangaroo and a
koala. They all act as a 1930s chorus and do a little*

enter down right

dance around ALEXANDER. Soon after the MOTHER
enters she presents ALEXANDER with an Australian
cowboy hat, which he puts on. It's got a sprig of euca-
lyptus in it.)

ALEXANDER (*sings*).
    I'm tired of being punched
    And pushed and smushed and scrunched.
    I'm packing up and moving to Australia.
    My life's a messy mess
    I'll never hear a yes
    Unless unless unless I move to Australia.

    Down Under. Down Under.
    They call Australia Down Under
    Because it's down below.
    When here it's freezing cold
    Australia's summer gold
    Makes folks forget there's such a thing as snow.

    No news that's not good news.
    Hip-hopping kangaroos.
    Koalas oozing love down in Australia:
    That's what I'm sure to find
    When I make up my mind
    To leave bad days behind and go go go
    To oh oh oh
    Au Au Au Australia.

    I will climb eucalyptus trees
    And run with the wallabies
    And do mostly what I please

    Whoa Whoa Whoa Whoa Whoa Whoa
    The day I finally go *move next to*
    The day I finally go to oh oh oh *alexander*
    Au Au Au Australia.

(Says.) I think I'm gonna move to Australia.

Segue to "AUSTRALIA" PLAY-OFF MUSIC (Dark) (12B)

(During the <u>light part</u> of the play-off music, ALEXAN-DER shadowboxes with the kangaroo, and gives the sprig of eucalyptus in his hat to the koala, who munches it while exiting. After everyone else leaves the stage, AL-EXANDER strides off.

Music immediately shifts to the darker part of the play-off music, which covers transition to dentist. NICK and ANTHONY enter with chairs to form the three-seat wait-ing room and a separate one-chair office. Music ends when dentist set-up is ready.

NICK and ANTHONY are standing in the office. PHILIP and PAUL sneak on and try to scare NICK and AN-THONY with their Novocain needle and drill routine, but the boys are unimpressed. They roll their eyes, and PHILIP and PAUL exit. Immediately, MOTHER and DR. FIELDS enter office.)

DR. FIELDS *(to MOTHER)*. Well, that's two for two. An-thony's mouth looks just as good as Nick's. Your boys are doing SOMETHING right. So, let's get Alexander in here and see if we can make it three for three. Alexander?

(ALEXANDER enters from offstage very very slowly, perhaps taking baby steps or doing some other maneuver to avoid getting there.)

MOTHER. Move it, Alexander. Dr. Fields doesn't have all day.

NICK. Yeah, Alexander, move your butt.

ANTHONY. He's scared.

NICK. Real scared.

ANTHONY. Maybe even terrified.

NICK. Definitely terrified. Definitely dragging his butt.

MOTHER. Nick, I'd like you to lose the word "butt" right now, and both of you, stop teasing Alexander, and Alexander, get your—tushie—in here this minute.

(ALEXANDER climbs into the dentist chair and promptly pulls his sweater up over his face.)

DR. FIELDS *(jocularly)*. Come out, come out, wherever you are.

(ALEXANDER turns around in his chair, kneeling in the seat, with his bottom facing DR. FIELDS.)

DR. FIELDS *(not so jocularly)*. I'll need you to turn around, please, Alexander.

(ALEXANDER turns around, and slides down in the chair so that his head is now in the seat.)

ANTHONY. What a fool!

NICK. What a—tushie—head!

MOTHER *(to NICK and ANTHONY)*. Boys, leave. *(They leave for the waiting room, which is away from the dentist chair. To ALEXANDER.)* Alexander, sit up. *(To DR. FIELDS.)* I think I'll get out of your way and let you do ... whatever you have to do.

(MOTHER joins BOYS in the waiting room where they're already seated, stops them from pummeling each other, and sits between them. DR. FIELDS pulls his mirror and pick—they should be over-sized—from his pocket. ALEXANDER sees them, clamps his mouth shut, and tries to scream the following words with his mouth closed.)

ALEXANDER. No! No no no! Let me out of here! Stop!

(In the waiting room, MOTHER and BOYS listen, not quite sure they heard anything serious.)

DR. FIELDS. Stop WHAT? We haven't started yet. First you have to open your mouth.

ALEXANDER *(opening his mouth a little)*. Uh. *(As soon as DR. FIELDS approaches with the instruments, however, he clamps his mouth shut and tries to scream, first with closed lips, then out of one side, then the other, of his mouth.)* Eeee. Aaaaah! Aaaaaaaah!

DR. FIELDS. Would you please open.

(ALEXANDER moans.)

DR. FIELDS. Wider, please.

(ALEXANDER moans louder.)

DR. FIELDS. Wider.

(ALEXANDER throws his mouth wide open, but as DR. FIELDS approaches with the instruments, he begins to shout.)

ALEXANDER. Save me. Somebody save me. Ooooh. Eeee. Ooooh. Ow. Ouch.

(DR. FIELDS has pulled away at the first sound, but AL-EXANDER carries on as if he's being tortured. MOTHER and the two BOYS jump up and pantomime listening at the wall.)

DR. FIELDS. I'm just looking around in your mouth, Alexander. *(Very slowly.)* Looking does not hurt.

(Upon hearing DR. FIELDS' voice, MOTHER is reassured and sits the BOYS back down. ALEXANDER decides to face the inevitable, braces himself in the chair and, somewhat like a sacrificial lamb, throws his head back with his mouth wide open. DR. FIELDS heaves a sigh and, with the instruments, looks around in ALEX-ANDER's mouth. After a moment:)

DR. FIELDS. Hmmmm.
ALEXANDER. Hmmmm? *(Panicking.)* What's hmmmm? *(Screams.)* H-e-e-l-l-l-p-p-p! *(MOTHER, NICK, and AN-THONY run in.)* He's hmmmmming me.
MOTHER. He's WHAT-ing you?

ALEXANDER. He's hmmmming me. I hate that hmmmm.

MOTHER *(inquiringly to DR. FIELDS)*. Hmmm?

DR. FIELDS *(to MOTHER)*. Yes, well, I'm afraid we only
scored two out of three today. No cavities for Anthony.
No cavities for Nick. But it looks like Alexander has a
cavity *(pauses and points)* back there.

MOTHER. Don't worry, sweetie. Dr. Fields will take care
of it.

DR. FIELDS. That's right. Come back next week, and I'll
get it all fixed up.

ALEXANDER. Next week I'm going to Australia.

*(MOTHER and DR. FIELDS look at ALEXANDER. AL-
EXANDER gets up from dentist chair as "AUSTRALIA"
PLAY-OFF MUSIC (12C) begins. DR. FIELDS and
MOTHER leave, taking the dentist chair off. TWO EN-
SEMBLE ACTORS enter to form an elevator. ANTHONY
presses the button, the doors open, and NICK and AN-
THONY get in. As ALEXANDER approaches, the doors
close on his foot, slamming on it repeatedly. "AUSTRA-
LIA" PLAY-OFF music fades out during foot slamming
bit. NICK and ANTHONY laugh, and ALEXANDER hops
to what is now the outside of the dentist's building, holding his foot as the actors playing the elevator "high-
five" each other and exit. ANTHONY and NICK push
ALEXANDER over onto the muddy ground. When he
stands up, they point at his clothes and laugh. They
freeze, he steps forward and addresses the audience.)*

ALEXANDER. On the way downstairs the elevator door
closed on my foot and while we were waiting for my
mom to go get the car Anthony made me fall where it

was muddy and then when I started crying because of the mud Nick said I was a—

NICK *(unfreezes)*. Crybaby. Crybaby. You're a little crybaby.

(ALEXANDER circles NICK with his fist clenched. NICK taunts him. ALEXANDER tucks his head down and goes at NICK, his fists pummeling like pistons. NICK puts his hand on ALEXANDER's forehead and easily holds him at arm's length so the fists do no harm. ANTHONY grabs ALEXANDER and pulls him off NICK. ALEXANDER is dead-serious about this fight, but his brothers are amused by it, and there is nothing really menacing in this scene.)

ALEXANDER. Get off me, Anthony, or you'll be sorry. You'll BOTH be sorry.

(ANTHONY thumbs his nose at ALEXANDER, and while ALEXANDER is looking at him trying to decide what to do, NICK kicks him in the bottom. ALEXANDER swings around, goes into a crouch, and tries to butt NICK in the stomach with his head. ANTHONY manages to catch ALEXANDER by the seat of his pants and keeps his head from ever connecting with NICK. ALEXANDER keeps trying, and NICK keeps jumping back out of his way and taunting him. It all stops as soon as MOTHER enters.)

MOTHER. Alexander, WHAT do you think you're doing?

ALEXANDER. I'm punching Nick in the stomach with my head. Because, because—

MOTHER. I don't want to hear any becauses. I leave you alone for five minutes, Alexander, five minutes, and you're fighting and you're muddy and *(she sighs and shakes her head)* and...well...if we're going to the shoe store we better get going, but I just don't understand you, Alexander. I don't understand what's got into you today.

(MOTHER exits, followed by NICK and ANTHONY.)

ALEXANDER *(calling to them).* I'm having a terrible, horrible, no good, very bad day. I having a terrible, horrible, no good, very bad day. I'm having— *(He now addresses the audience, encouraging them to join in.)* —maybe they can't hear me; come on, help me—a TERRIBLE, HORRIBLE, NO GOOD, VERY BAD DAY. *(ALEXANDER puts his finger up to his lips to silence the audience. He listens for a response from his family before saying:)* No one even answered. *(ALEXANDER exits.)*

("SHOES" MUSIC (13A) begins as the SHOE SALESMAN enters and sets up three chairs to form a bench. As soon as it is ready, NICK, ANTHONY, and ALEXANDER enter, pantomime looking at all the wonderful racks of shoes, and throw themselves onto the bench. "SHOES" music ends. MOTHER enters.)

ANTHONY. I want those white sneakers with the blue stripes I saw in the window.

NICK. And I want the red ones with the white stripes.

MOTHER. Please, boys. How about a little please.

ANTHONY & NICK (*together*). Please.

ALEXANDER. And I want the blue ones with the red stripes, please please please please please. (*Looks around.*) Gee, Mr. Shoe Man. You've sure got a lot of shoes in this store.

SALESMAN (*says*). Yeah, I've got shoes.

(*MUSIC—"SHOES" (13B) starts, plays under next two lines and leads into SALESMAN starting the song.*)

ALEXANDER. For kids AND for grownups.

SALESMAN (*says*). All kinds of shoes.

(*Sings, doing some choreographed steps and gestures.*)
> **Good-looking shoes.**
> **Hot-hot-hot-hot shoes.**
>
> **Boots for when it's raining.**
> **Sandals for the sun.**
> **Shoes for when you're chilling out and when you**
> **   want to run.**
> **Softball and soccer and Kung Fu and Michael**
> **   Jordan shoes.**
>
> **Amazing shoes.**
> **Awesome shoes.**
> **Yeah, I've got shoes.**
> **Hot-hot-hot-hot shoes.**
>
> **Tap shoes.**
> **Toe shoes.**
> **Seven-feet-deep snow shoes.**

High shoes.
Low shoes.
Ready, set, and go shoes.
Shoes.
Awesome shoes.
Hey, I've got shoes.
Hot-hot-hot-hot shoes.
Slippers for your bathrobes.
Loafers for your ties.
Cowboy boots that make you taller than the other
guys.

MOTHER *(sings alone)*.
Red, green, blue, and orange,
Pink, purple, gold, and silver shoes.

MOTHER & SALESMAN *(sing, doing some choreographed
moves together)*.
Good-looking shoes.
Amazing shoes.
All kinds of shoes.
Hot-hot-hot-hot shoes.

*(The song now develops into a full-scale production
number. The remaining TWO ENSEMBLE ACTORS
come out as shoe helpers and in the course of the dance
help NICK and ANTHONY change from their old shoes
into their new. ALEXANDER does not get his new ones
yet.)*

MOTHER *(sings alone)*.
> Sweet shoes.
> Baaad shoes.
> Dancing with your dad shoes.
> Plain shoes.
> Plaid shoes.

ALEXANDER *(says)*. Very very mad shoes.

EVERYONE *(sings)*.
> Shoes.
> Awesome shoes.
> Yeah, he's got shoes.
> Hot-hot-hot-hot shoes.

ALEXANDER *(sings alone)*.
> Shoes you close with Velcro.
> Shoes you lace up tight.
> Shoes that stay exactly where you took them off
>   last night.
> Jumping, jungle-gymming, rock-climbing,
>   even swimming shoes.

NICK & ANTHONY *(sing)*.
> Amazing shoes.
> All kinds of shoes.
> Yeah, he's got shoes.
> Hot-hot-hot-hot shoes.

NICK *(sings alone)*.
> Shoes you mess around in.
> Shoes you must keep clean.

ANTHONY *(sings).*
>   Shoes you use to step on brothers when you're
>   feeling mean.

ANTHONY AND NICK *(sing).*
>   Kickboxing, cartwheeling, maybe walking on the
>   ceiling shoes.

EVERYONE *(sings).*
>   Good-looking shoes.
>   Awesome shoes.
>   All kinds of shoes

SALESMAN *(sings alone).*
>   Hot-hot-hot-hot shoes.
>
>   Brown shoes.
>   Black shoes.
>   To the moon and back shoes.
>   Silk shoes.
>   Suede shoes.
>   Stay dry when you wade shoes.
>   Tough shoes.
>   Soft shoes.
>   Stay on when you cough shoes.
>   Huge shoes.
>   Small shoes.
>   Yeah, I've got them all shoes.

(As we go for the big finish, EVERYONE is dancing, and the SHOE HELPERS dance with shoes on their hands, so it looks as if the shoes are dancing in the air.)

EVERYONE *(sings)*.
>**Shoes.**
>**Amazing shoes.**
>**Awesome shoes.**
>**Good-looking shoes.**
>**Hot-hot-hot-hot shoes.**

SALESMAN *(sings alone)*.
>**Yeah, I've got shoes.**

EVERYONE *(sings)*.
>**Yeah, he's got shoes.**
>**Hot, hot, hot, hot, hot, hot shoes.**

SALESMAN *(sings alone)*.
>**Yeah, shoes.**

(At the end of the number, the SHOE SALESMAN sends off his HELPERS. He turns to the BOYS.)

SALESMAN. So, let's see what we have here. Yours are the white sneakers with the blue stripes, I believe, and they fit— *(He checks the fit.)* —great!

ANTHONY. Awesome.

NICK. Hot-hot-hot-hot.

ALEXANDER. Mine'll be hotter.

SALESMAN *(turns to NICK)*. And here are your red sneakers with the white stripes and they are— *(He checks the toes.)* —perfect.

(NICK bops around triumphantly, doing a thumbs-up with both hands.)

ALEXANDER. Mine'll be perfecter.

SALESMAN. Yes, so, I believe you wanted the blue sneakers with the red stripes?

ALEXANDER. Yeah. They're the hottest.

SALESMAN. They may well be, but I'm afraid we only have them in smaller sizes.

ALEXANDER (*collapses with disappointment but quickly revives*). So give me a smaller size. I can wear a smaller size. I'll just scrunch up my toes a little and—

MOTHER. I don't think so, sweetie. Why don't you find something else you like?

(*ALEXANDER walks over to the imaginary display and pantomimes checking out various sneakers.*)

ALEXANDER. Okay, I'll take the green with the yellow stripes.

SALESMAN. Sorry, no stripes in your size. I've already checked.

ALEXANDER. Then those high-top orange ones. I like them too.

SALESMAN. No high tops in your size. No orange in your size. Actually, no colors in your size.

(*ALEXANDER flops down disconsolately on the bench.*)

SALESMAN. But I do have these ...

(*He gestures and the SHOE HELPERS enter, carrying a fantastically decorated shoebox as triumphal "PRESENTATION" MUSIC (13C) plays. The music stops when the salesman finishes his flourishes and speaks.*)

SALESMAN (*opening the box with a great flourish*).
  WHITE ones!
ALEXANDER. Never. Not ever. No way. Uh uh. N.O.

(*MOTHER glances at her watch, then gestures to the
SALESMAN, and the two of them kneel to put the shoes
on ALEXANDER.*)

NICK (*taking pity on ALEXANDER*). They're okay, Alex-
  ander. Really.
ALEXANDER. Absolutely, positively no.
ANTHONY (*also taking pity*). Hey, white's kind of ... hot.
NICK. Yeah, white's all right.

ANTHONY & NICK (*chanting in unison*).
    White's all right.
    White's all right.
    White's all—

(*MOTHER puts up her hand to silence the chanting.*)

SALESMAN. Fits like a glove.
ALEXANDER. I hate them.
MOTHER. We'll take them.

(*ALEXANDER and MOTHER glare at each other for a
moment, and then she exits. SALESMAN, ANTHONY,
NICK, and the SHOE HELPERS take off the shoe-store
chairs as ALEXANDER steps forward and addresses the
audience.*)

ALEXANDER. They made me buy plain old white ones—
(Taking off his new shoes and glaring at the audience.)
—but they can't make me wear them.
MOTHER *(offstage)*. Come on, Alexander, let's go.

exit down right

*("SHOES" PLAY-OFF MUSIC (13D) begins as ALEX-
ANDER, in stocking feet, stomps off the stage. When he
gets backstage he changes into his old shoes. Segue to
"COPIER" MUSIC (14) to cover transition to the office
scene. TWO ENSEMBLE ACTORS appear with the large
rolling copy machine.)*

ENSEMBLE #3. Presenting...
ENSEMBLE #3 & #4 *(together)*. The Okidoki 2000!!!

*(They move it across stage. Lights on the copy machine
flash. The TWO ENSEMBLE ACTORS, whom we will
now call the OFFICE GENIES, signal to the sides, and
the rest of the cast assemble the office: the table, now
serving as a desk, with a large computer and piles of
books on it, and three chairs, one behind the desk, one
next to it, and one at the side of the copy machine. When
the office is set, the OFFICE GENIES go to the sides of
the copy machine and begin to make "electronic" beep-
ing noises. Still making the noises, they withdraw behind
and into the copy machine, where they are well-hidden
except when they stick their heads up. These two OF-
FICE GENIES are responsible for all the movements
and sounds of the inanimate objects of the office, and
ultimately for getting ALEXANDER in trouble. No one
ever acknowledges their presence in the office.)*

The copy machine noises fade and the lights stop flash-
ing as FATHER enters from one side with his briefcase,
and MOTHER and the BOYS enter from the other. FA-
THER sets his briefcase down on the chair next to his
desk, and FATHER and MOTHER kiss. MUSIC ends.)

FATHER. Hi, honey. Hi, guys. Thanks for picking me up.
So how did it go at the dentist?

ANTHONY. No cavities.

NICK. No cavities.

ALEXANDER. Cavity.

FATHER. Sorry about that, Alexander. *(To MOTHER.)* Just
give me a few more minutes to finish up here and I'll be
ready to leave. *(Sits down at desk.)*

MOTHER. Sounds good. We'll wait in the outer office.

NICK *(to ANTHONY)*. I'll play you tic-tac-toe.

ALEXANDER *(to ANTHONY)*. Play me, too.

ANTHONY. You're too easy to beat. Let's go, Nick.

(NICK and ANTHONY and MOTHER exit. ALEXANDER
stays. FATHER turns back to his work, while ALEXAN-
DER prowls around the office. Suddenly the copy ma-
chine lights flash as the machine makes its electronic
noises, and moves into ALEXANDER's path.)

ALEXANDER. What's this big thing?

FATHER *(lifting his head from his work)*. It's the new
copying machine. And it's strictly hands off, okay?

(FATHER turns back to his work and ALEXANDER ex-
amines the copier. He starts with his hands behind his

back. *The machine's noises seem to be tempting him to touch it.*)

ALEXANDER. This is cool. (*The machine's noises seem to agree.*) I bet it can make a hundred copies. (*The machine's noises seem to suggest that it can make many more.*) Maybe a thousand. (*Keep going, the machine seems to say.*) Maybe even a million. (*Now you're talking, the noises seem to tell him.*)

(*The temptation is too much for ALEXANDER. He sneaks a paper out of his father's briefcase, climbs on the chair next to the copier, and puts the paper in the copier. He climbs down from the chair and presses lots of buttons. The machine, making its noises, begins to produce copies, slowly at first, but growing faster and faster while its noises grow louder and louder. It begins spitting paper out in a stream. [Actually the OFFICE GENIES are shoving the paper out through a slit in the copier's side.] ALEXANDER tries to stop the outpouring of paper, but he only succeeds in getting paper all over the room. The commotion finally attracts his father's attention.*)

FATHER (*leaping from his desk chair*). No! Alexander, no!

(*FATHER rushes over to the machine and pushes buttons fruitlessly until he hits the right one and the machine stops. He looks at ALEXANDER, who is busy trying to stuff the paper back into the machine or up inside his shirt.*)

FATHER (*sternly*). Did I or didn't I tell you not to play with the copier?

ALEXANDER. Did.

FATHER. And were you or weren't you playing with it?

ALEXANDER. Weren't.

FATHER. Weren't? What do you mean, weren't?

ALEXANDER. I weren't—I mean I wasn't—PLAYING with it. I was...I was...TESTING it. To see if it's working okay. And it is. It's working real good.

FATHER (*highly exasperated*). Away from the machine, Alexander. Now.

(*FATHER returns to his desk and his work, while ALEXANDER glares at the copy machine, its lights and sounds seeming to laugh at him as it moves back to where it belongs. ALEXANDER turns his back on it and looks around for something to do. "BORED-DANCE" MUSIC (15) plays as he tries different ways of hopping and jumping, finally settling on a walk that involves swinging his elbows far to the sides. The OFFICE GENIES pop out from behind the copy machine and move to the stack of books. ALEXANDER is getting dangerously close to that very same stack.*)

FATHER (*looking up from his work*). Watch out for that stack of books, Alexan—

(*It's too late. ALEXANDER's elbow has swatted the stack, and the GENIES make sure the books topple onto the floor. MUSIC ends as books tumble.*)

FATHER. Oh, for Pete's sake! I don't BELIEVE this!

(NICK, ANTHONY, and MOTHER come rushing back in. FATHER points mutely to the books on the floor and to the general mess ALEXANDER has made.)

ALEXANDER. I was careful as could be, except for my elbow.

FATHER. Out. Could everyone please go out *(He points to outer office.)* there?

MOTHER. Okay, boys. Back to the outer office till your dad's done.

(While NICK leaves and MOTHER and FATHER aren't looking, ANTHONY threatens ALEXANDER with his fist and then leaves. ALEXANDER quickly kneels to tie a shoelace.)

MOTHER. You too, Alexander. You ESPECIALLY.

ALEXANDER. I'm just tying my laces. I'll be right there.

(MOTHER and FATHER exchange a look. MOTHER exits, but FATHER keeps his eye on ALEXANDER. Suddenly, ONE OF THE OFFICE GENIES gets FATHER's attention back to his computer with an electronic-sounding message:)

OFFICE GENIE. Beep! You've got mail!

(FATHER returns to work at his desk. ALEXANDER is done with his shoe and is just about to leave the office, however reluctantly, when his attention is drawn to his father's briefcase. FATHER, unaware of this new menace, continues working.

ALEXANDER stalks the briefcase as if he were a panther. "CELL PHONE" MUSIC (16) begins. He pulls the chair with the briefcase on it in front of him at center stage, and opens it to inspect its contents. The OFFICE GENIES observe his progress with evil approval. Music ends when ALEXANDER delivers next line.)

ALEXANDER. My dad's got so much good stuff in his briefcase.

(He removes the contents, one by one, and checks them out. As each briefcase item is checked out, the OFFICE GENIES pop up from behind the copy machine and look at each other, reacting silently to the item's potential for trouble, and then popping back down till the next item appears. The words in parentheses are indications of the GENIES' reactions but should not be spoken.)

ALEXANDER. Address book.

(genies—Nah!)

ALEXANDER. Notebook.

(genies—Nah!)

ALEXANDER. Calculator.

(genies—Maybe.)

ALEXANDER. Oh, cool. His cell phone.

(genies—Bingo!)

(The OFFICE GENIES "high-five" and disappear behind the copy machine.)

ALEXANDER *(to FATHER)*. Hey, Dad, do you take your cell phone everywhere? Like to bed? In the shower? When you're on the—?
FATHER *(looking up and speaking very firmly)*. Put down my phone. Tie your shoes. Go.

(FATHER turns back to his work and ALEXANDER reluctantly puts the cell phone back in the briefcase. It beeps at him—the VOICE OF ONE OF THE OFFICE GENIES, of course. ALEXANDER picks the phone back up and looks at it, then at the audience as if to say, "Is it talking to me?" Then he shakes his head and puts it back down. It beeps again. He looks at it again, and again at the audience, as if to say, "Is it asking me to?" He shakes his head and puts it back down. It beeps a third time. ALEXANDER picks it back up. The temptation is too great. He maniacally punches in many, many numbers. The phone beeps, then rings. We hear a voice with an Australian accent—It's ONE OF THE OFFICE GENIES:)

OFFICE GENIE. Hello, g'day, mate.
ALEXANDER. Wow!
FATHER *(looking up, alarmed)*. What?

(From the phone we hear, in an Australian accent:)

OFFICE GENIE. Hello, I'm in the outback. Who's there?
ALEXANDER. I think I called Australia.

(From the phone we hear, in an Australian accent:)

OFFICE GENIE. That's right, mate. Oooh—there goes a 'roo!

(FATHER jumps up, grabs the phone from ALEXAN-DER, and wildly presses buttons until the call is disconnected. He looks around for ALEXANDER, who is trying to sneak away.)

FATHER. Uh-uh-uh-uh. Come here, Alexander.

(ALEXANDER returns. FATHER places his hands on ALEXANDER's shoulders and looks him in the face. AL-EXANDER, abashed, is hanging his head.)

FATHER. Now listen carefully. It's nice of you, and your brothers, and mom to come pick me up at the office. But *(Very slowly and with exasperated patience.)* please... don't... pick... me... up... anymore.

("AUSTRALIA"—FINAL PLAY-OFF MUSIC (17) starts. ALEXANDER exits. FATHER shakes his head and exits, taking his briefcase. ENSEMBLE ACTORS enter to clear the office furniture. The OFFICE GENIES step out from behind the copy machine and congratulate each other. Perhaps they take a bow. ALEXANDER re-enters and glares at the copy machine as the OFFICE GENIES wheel it offstage, perhaps saying again, after music fades:)

ENSEMBLE #3. The Okidoki ...
ENSEMBLE #4. 2000.

ALEXANDER (*crossing downstage and addressing audience directly*). Okay, let's do it. It was a terrible, horrible, no good, very bad day. (*He leads the audience in the increasingly louder chant.*) It was a terrible ... horrible ... no good ... very bad ... day. It was a terrible ... horrible ... no good ... very bad ... day.

(*By the third time, TWO ENSEMBLE ACTORS have arrived with ALEXANDER's bed quilt, which they hold in front of ALEXANDER as he changes clothes, his head popping up whenever he speaks to the audience.*)

ALEXANDER. There were lima beans for dinner and I hate limas. EECCH!!! (*His head disappears behind the quilt as he starts changing clothes, and then pops back up.*) There was kissing on TV and I hate kissing. EEUWWW!!! (*His head again disappears behind the quilt, then pops back up.*) My bath was too hot. OUCH!!! (*Disappears, pops back up.*) I got soap in my eyes. AARRGH! (*Disappears, pops back up.*) My marble went down the drain. OH NO! (*Disappears, pops back up*). And ... I had to wear my railroad-train pajamas.

(*With the delivery of the railroad-train pajamas line, the TWO ENSEMBLE ACTORS drop the quilt, revealing ALEXANDER in the hated pajamas. MOTHER enters and picks up the quilt.*)

ALEXANDER (*to MOTHER*). I hate my railroad-train pajamas.

MOTHER. I know you do, sweetie, but all the others were in the wash. Now come on, I'll go up with you. Time for bed.

(The ENSEMBLE ACTORS roll on ALEXANDER's bed, and MOTHER lays out the quilt on it.)

ALEXANDER. I hate time for bed.

(NICK enters Alexander's bedroom and grabs one of his pillows off the bed.)

ALEXANDER. Hey, give me back that pillow.
NICK. It's my pillow.
ALEXANDER. But you said I could use it.
NICK. Well, now I say you can't.

(ALEXANDER grabs for the pillow and he and NICK have a brief, silent tug-of-war. NICK wins and exits, carrying the pillow. MOTHER looks after NICK with disapproval.)

ALEXANDER. I hate it when Nick takes back his pillow. *(He starts jumping up and down on his bed.)* And I hate my white sneakers. And I hate Dr. Fields finding a cavity just in me.
MOTHER *(getting him back down on the bed)*. Okay, sweetie, just settle down and I'll turn on your Mickey Mouse night-light.

(ONE OF THE ENSEMBLE ACTORS enters with the night-light. MOTHER flicks the switch a couple of times

but it won't light. The ENSEMBLE ACTOR shrugs and walks off.)

MOTHER. Oh, dear, I guess it burned out.

ALEXANDER *(starting to jump again).* I hate it when my night-light burns out. And I hate it that you forgot to put in dessert. And I—ooh, owww, ooooo. *(ALEXANDER sinks onto his bed, clutching his mouth.)*

MOTHER. What? What did you do?

ALEXANDER. Oooo. Owwww. I bit my tongue. I hate biting my tongue.

ANTHONY *(entering with NICK).* Hey, Alexander, we're playing find the cat.

NICK. Yeah, and guess where we found him?

ALEXANDER. He's supposed to be here. He's supposed to be sleeping with me.

NICK. Not tonight he isn't. He's already sound asleep in Anthony's bed.

(The two BOYS run off. MOTHER shakes her head.)

ALEXANDER *(to MOTHER).* I hate THAT, too. And I hate that I woke up with gum in my hair. And I hate that I'm not Paul's best friend anymore. And I hate that we had lima beans for supper. And I hate—

MOTHER *(sitting at the edge of ALEXANDER's bed and trying to console him).* My goodness, Alexander. My goodness. You HAVE had a bad day.

ALEXANDER. Uh HUH.

MOTHER. A REALLY bad day.

ALEXANDER. Double uh huh.

MOTHER. Double uh huh is right. But I'll tell you something. This day is almost done.

ALEXANDER. So?

MOTHER. So you get to start all over again tomorrow. And I'm sure tomorrow will be a better day.

ALEXANDER. Maybe it'll be worse.

MOTHER. No, I think it'll be better.

ALEXANDER. Promise?

MOTHER. I can't PROMISE promise. But that's what I think. And that's what I hope. And that's what I wish.

(MUSIC "THE SWEETEST OF NIGHTS AND THE FINEST OF DAYS" INTRO AND SONG (18). The intro plays under "And that's what I wish" and continues through "Oh, yes," then leads into MOTHER singing.)

ALEXANDER. That's what you wish?

MOTHER Oh, yes.

(Sings.)
> I wish you,
> I wish you these wishes:
> Cool drinks in your glasses.
> Warm food in your dishes.
> People to nourish, and cherish, and love you.

(As MOTHER sings, FATHER enters. ALEXANDER sees him and is afraid he's in for a scolding. Instead, FATHER gives ALEXANDER a hug. ALEXANDER hugs back.)

MOTHER *(sings).*

> A lamp in the window to light your way home
>   in the haze.
> I wish you the sweetest of nights and the finest of
>   days.

(As the music plays, FATHER joins MOTHER and gives her a hug. NICK and ANTHONY enter, playfully tossing the pillow back and forth. ALEXANDER sulks, left out of the game. MOTHER notices, and the BOYS stop their game as she sings.)

> I wish you, I wish you
> A talent for living.
> Delight in the getting.
> Delight in the giving.

(NICK and ANTHONY give ALEXANDER the pillow and punch him playfully.)

> A song in your soul, and someone to hear it.
> The wisdom to find the right path when
>   you're lost in a maze.
> I wish you the sweetest of nights and the finest of
>   days.

(At words "lost in a maze" FATHER, NICK, and ANTHONY move to the corners of the bed and move the bed in a complete sweeping arc around the stage, the bed-moving beginning with the words "finest of days" and ending before the following words are begun.)

know when to start,

MOTHER (*sings*).
    A snug roof above you.
    A strong self inside you.
    The courage to go where you know you must go
    And a good heart to guide you.
    And good friends beside you.

(*PHILIP and PAUL enter. They give ALEXANDER the special friendship handshake. ALL sing harmony under MOTHER's song. FATHER joins MOTHER on bed.*)

    I wish you, I wish you
    A dream worth the doing.
    And fortune's face smiling
    On all you're pursuing.
    And pleasures that far far outweigh your small
        sorrows.
    Arms opened wide to embrace your tomorrows.
    A long sunlit sail on the bluest and smoothest of
        bays.
    I wish you the sweetest of nights and the finest of
        days.

(*After the word "tomorrows" PHILIP, PAUL, AN-THONY, and NICK move to the corners of the bed and move it in a sweeping figure eight around the stage, with ALEXANDER on his knees at one end, his arms raised triumphantly as if he's the prow of the ship. Bed stops moving when "finest of days" is sung.*)

As the song winds down, MOTHER starts tenderly tucking ALEXANDER in as FATHER kisses the other BOYS good night.)

MOTHER *(sings).*
I wish you the sweetest of nights and the finest of days.

add music

ALEXANDER *(speaking as he settles in).* Well, maybe tomorrow WILL be better. But today— *(Sighs.)* —today— It's been a terrible, horrible, no good, very bad day. *(His head is now on the pillow.)*

MOTHER. It sure has. But you know what?

ALEXANDER *(pops back up).* What?

MOTHER *(settling him back down again).* Some days are like that.

ALEXANDER *(pops up again and looks at his parents).* Even in Australia?

MOTHER *(as she settles him back down).* Even in Australia.

(FATHER and MOTHER exit, arm in arm.

"AUSTRALIA"—FINALE MUSIC (19) starts. ALEXANDER pops up, sees the kangaroo and koala bear peeking in. He makes room for them in the bed, and as they snuggle with him he gives the audience a thumbs-up, and settles down to sleep. Music ends as ALEXANDER falls asleep. Lights fade to black.)

THE (FIRST) END

(Lights come up and the CAST sings "IF I WERE IN CHARGE OF THE WORLD" SONG (20)—last verse only.)

EVERYONE *(sings).*
>   If I were in charge of the world
>   A chocolate sundae with whipped cream and nuts
>   would be a vegetable.
>   And every kind of movie would be G.

EVERYONE EXCEPT PARENTS *(sings).*
>   And a person who sometimes forgot to brush,
>   And sometimes forgot to flush,

EVERYONE *(sings).*
>   Would still be allowed to be
>   Would still be allowed to be
>   Would still be allowed to be
>   In charge of the world.

THE (FINAL) END

WHAT PEOPLE ARE SAYING about *Alexander and the Terrible, Horrible, No Good, Very Bad Day*...

"Delightfully funny! The show sold out almost as soon as we advertised it."

Carey Cahoon,
Palace Professional Children's Theatre, Manchester, N.H.

"*Alexander*... is an entertaining musical—tremendously popular with young ones—most of whom know the original by heart. Very faithful and very funny—a huge success for our children's theatre."

Chuck Minsker, First Stage Theater Company,
Huntington, W.V.

"*Alexander*... is a sure-fire audience-pleaser. With its delightful tunes and fun characters, it is a show that reaches all age groups from pre-K to grownups. Our audiences loved it!"

Julie Condy, Stage to Stage Inc., New Orleans, La.

DIRECTOR'S NOTES

DIRECTOR'S NOTES

DIRECTOR'S NOTES